Teodora
Hugs & kisses
RJ Scott ♡

Deefur Dog

RJ Scott
Copyright 2011 by RJ Scott
Print Edition: August 2013

Cover design by Meredith Russell

RJ Scott

All Rights Reserved

This literary work may not be reproduced or transmitted in any form or by any means, including electronic or photographic reproduction, in whole or in part, without express written permission. This book cannot be copied in any format, sold, or otherwise transferred from your computer to another through upload to a file sharing peer to peer program, for free or for a fee. Such action is illegal and in violation of Copyright Law.

Deefur Dog

Dedication

To my dad, who was taken from us so many years ago now. It was his bi-weekly library trip, his love for books, and him lending me his library ticket, that took me from Enid Blyton in the kids' area to the wonders of Tolkein in the adult shelves.

To Steve, a wonderful dad. Happy Father's Day from 'me and the kids'... all four of us. xxx

Trademarks Acknowledgement

The author acknowledges the trademarked status and trademark owners of the following wordmarks mentioned in this work of fiction:

Barney the Dinosaur: HiT Entertainment
Disney: The Walt Disney Company
Minnie Mouse: The Walt Disney Company
Tide: Procter & Gamble
Toyota: Toyota Motor Corporation

Deefur Dog

Chapter 1

"That's an impossible deadline," Cameron Jackson snapped, aware of the frustration and exhaustion running through his voice. *So much for staying calm* he thought. He shifted the phone to his other ear, balancing his fractious daughter on one hip and pushing his Great Dane away with his other. He tried to concentrate on what his brother and business partner said but found it damn near impossible above the noise of barking dog and over-tired sobbing daughter.

"Dadda, wan' chocca," Emma whined, tears in her eyes, her small hands twisted in his hair, pulling just this side of painful. He wished one more time she would give in and have her nap. He needed an hour — only an hour — to make some decisions, to actually get some vital work done.

"Shhh, baby, Daddy's on the phone," he muttered, trying to jiggle his hip without losing hold of the phone clamped between his shoulder and ear.

"Cam?"

"Not you, sorry — I have Emma here — "

"I thought your new nanny — Elsa or

something—y'know, the one with the mauve hair, was working well?" Cameron winced at the evidence of a mix of surprise and disappointment in Neal's words

And therein lay the problem. Yet again, for another one of those highly reasonable reasons his nannies gave, he and his daughter had been left in the lurch. Elsa "Purple Rinse" Saunders, highly recommended by the agency as being able to manage the most fractured and difficult of households, had lasted exactly three days.

"It was fine until Emma realized her mauve hair was actually a wig and pulled it off." The mousy brown curls thus revealed had looked okay to Cameron, but Elsa had pitched a fit. "Em gave it to Deefur who buried the damn thing in the garden." And Elsa had pitched another fit. He sighed, wishing he could see the humor even as Neal snorted down the phone. "She left yesterday."

"Jeez, Cam, I can't believe you let Deefur anywhere near her. I thought we talked about this?"

"I didn't let him. He got out of the boot room somehow."

"What? He can open locked doors now?"

"No, Neal," Cam had to rein his natural

7

Deefur Dog

instinct for sarcasm, "he cannot open locked doors, I think the dog walker must have—I haven't got time for this. All you need to know is she said it 'was an impossible working environment' or some excuse—said she loved Emma but she couldn't..." his throat tightened with emotion, "and then she just left." The need to absolve himself of responsibility for her leaving asserted the urge for a fight. He needed to take his frustration out on someone, why not his baby brother? God knows since everything had hit the fan his brother had borne the brunt of his bad temper, on the job and off. Neal was used to it by now.

"Could you not have—" God, Neal is insistent.

"I didn't ask Emma to pull the wig off, or for Deefur to bury it."

"Okay. Okay... devil's advocate here bro— is you being pissed at the world in general the reason why you think we can't meet this new deadline?"

"No, it isn't the freaking reason!" Cameron swore. Immediate guilt filtered through him at cussing in front of his daughter, disappearing as soon as Deefur tried to push past him. He leaned harder against the dog to get him to stop rooting through the newly delivered groceries still sitting in piles by the door. A cabbage rolled tantalizingly around the floor just out of Deefur's reach. The sable haired Great Dane, easily the size of a small pony, pushed back, whining low in his throat, clearly wanting the damn cabbage. "Look, this is Adamson playing us off against the others. Neither of the rival bids they *say* they have, are gonna hit the target any more than we can. Certainly not without further off-plan changes, so whatever they threaten, they would be stupid to take the project elsewhere. We're two months into this. Why go out of state for a local job? It's not as if asking for bids from Seattle will be any better than what they get here in homegrown Tacoma."

Cam winced at the analogy although not an exceptionally good one. Tacoma was not a small town with one set of traffic signals, but a freaking urban Washington city. The third largest in the state in fact; a port hub and located right on the Puget Sound, and an area teeming with local color and history. Cam and Neal both believed strongly when customers wanted new builds, they wanted people who lived in Tacoma and had a feel for the work that needed doing. Someone who could design and build sympathetically, not some fly-by-night

Deefur Dog

construction company without heart.

"Still, the threat is there, Cam, and to be fair…" Neal's voice tailed off. The brothers had been having this conversation on and off for months now and Cameron braced himself for the continued hurt. "I want to make this easier for you. Bro, I don't think your eye is on the ball here. Maybe we should re-evaluate things?"

"Re-evaluate what? This is *our* company; you shouldn't have to shoulder all the responsibility."

"Listen C, I said I wouldn't blame you if you needed a break from all this. You're grieving and you're going to make yourself ill." Neal's brutal honesty was delivered in the way only a family member could do. Cam appreciated how his brother had his back. Neal would, and could, run their thriving construction company on his own if push came to shove.

"No. Just—no." The company grounded him, and he refused to give up the only thing appearing to be working right. Besides, Neal warranted more from Cameron on a personal level and certainly more in the business as co-owners. He deserved someone who pulled his weight, whatever the stresses and strains in his life.

"Dadda…" Emma had a particular whine in her voice only a tired toddler could pull off to perfection. The right amount of cute mixed in with a teaspoon of impatience and a pint of attention-seeking monster. He shushed and jiggled her gently, allowing Deefur to move, because his leg alone could not hold back one hundred and forty pounds of dog intent on some great cabbage-eating adventure in the hallway. Half closing his eyes and shaking his head, he watched Deefur pounce on the cabbage with all the agility of a ten-week-old puppy, wide jaws closing around the vegetable with ease. *Bang goes vegetables for dinner.* Cam sighed. Neal continued talking, only now he had moved on to super-sympathetic-brother speak which Cam hated.

"It's not been long—"

Cameron reacted instantly. "Nearly two years, Neal, I'm fine." He wanted to stop this train of conversation at the source, not prepared, yet again, to go through all the whys and wherefores of his being a widower.

"You *need* a nanny, Cam. You can't keep letting them slip through your fingers."

"I didn't *let* her," he huffed irritated. Was Neal not listening here? "She hated Deefur, she refused to feed Emma fruit yogurt, and didn't

Deefur Dog

approve of my *lifestyle*," he listed her faults quickly, shushing Emma when his raised voice started her whimpering into his neck.

"How the hell did she find out about your lifestyle? Did you tell her?" Neal used the same old argument, allowing sadness to overwhelm the rising temper. Neal counted himself as Cam's greatest supporter, but sometimes he could be so obtuse.

"There's pictures of us all over the damn house, what do you want me to do? Put away all the images of me and Mark? Of Mark with Emma? I'm not concealing who I am, and I am not hiding the man I loved from view."

"Cam—"

"Anyway, she turned out to be worse than useless. Deefur never liked her, wouldn't let her within five feet of him from day one."

"Deefur? Shit, Cam. He's a freaking dog. His opinion—"

"Dogs know."

"The dog you shouldn't even still have."

"He's Mark's dog." A simple statement, filled with all the emotion for what this meant. Quickly he realized what he had said. "Was Mark's—he's my dog—our dog. Emma's dog…" He tripped over his words and his voice tailed off in a hopeless way, the result of not really knowing how to defend what he had started to say. Yes, Mark had brought Deefur home as a puppy. Yes, Mark had the idea to have a dog, but Deefur was the family pet, Cam's and Emma's.

"He's an extra in your house you don't need." Neal had said this before and would undoubtedly say it again. "We talked about this. You need to get him re-homed. Make your life easier and put him up for adoption—"

"You want me to put Emma up for adoption as well?" The irrational response spilled from his lips before he could gather his thoughts. What did Neal want him to say? It seemed that the nannies would use any excuse they wanted, be it about him being gay, or Emma having an unconventional surrogacy birth, or having to deal with Deefur. All reasons why not one nanny lasted more than a few days.

"I never said you should put Emma up for adoption." Neal sounded way past hurt and Cameron grimaced. He had been way out of line. No one could question Neal's love for Emma, and Cameron didn't know why he had said what he had.

"I know. I'm sorry." Cameron let out another noisy exhalation and continued louder

Deefur Dog

over the sound of crunching cabbage and snuffly woofing. "The Agency said they were sending someone else over. She should be here soon." Even as he said the words, the sound of the doorbell startled him, and he stumble-tripped over a family size box of Tide, righting himself with a shoulder against the wall and exclaiming down the phone, "She's here!" A flood of relief nearly overwhelmed him.

Deefur did his infamous imitation of what Mark had always called his '*The Hound of the Baskervilles* imitation'; hurling himself at the door and baying like a lunatic. The whole door frame shook as the huge dog repeatedly tried to reach the person on the other side, pieces of cabbage being flung from his open jaws. The sudden barking started Emma off again with pitiful and very wet sobs into his neck, while she choked out "Daddy" and "chocca" over and over and over and —

"I'll call you back," he shouted down the phone to Neal, ignoring the faint, *what the hell?* before he disconnected the call.

Cameron lunged for the door, trying to pull back Deefur and at the same time not squeeze Emma to death in the current forty-five degree hold he had on her. He reached the handle past the confusing mess of panting, barking, swirling, jumping fur, and opened the door.

Only to see a small Toyota screeching away from the sidewalk in front of his house. He couldn't believe his eyes, looking up and down the deserted street to check again. Surely the woman leaving in the car couldn't be the last nanny on the agency books, leaving as soon as she'd arrived? His heart sank when the truth of what had happened hit home, and sudden, furious, self-pitying thoughts squirmed into his head. Damn it. Another prospective nanny bites the dust. This time Deefur was well and truly to blame; damned nanny didn't even get past the threshold.

"Chocca Dadda pwease?" Emma continued to squeeze out more tears as Deefur shouldered past them both to stand at the tall fence in the front yard, barking heroically at the retreating car. Thank God the escaping woman had shut the gate; otherwise, there would have been another trip to rescue Deefur from the pound after he chased the car clear across Tacoma.

"Chocca," he said helplessly to his clinging daughter, ignoring the disapproving looks from Mr Perkins at number fifteen, and shouting over the barking to get Deefur back indoors. Deefur showed no sign of stopping the deep and frantic baying. From Deefur's point of view, the

Deefur Dog

perceived intruder needed to be well and truly told off.

Deefur snorted and let out a few extra *oofing* barks, almost under his breath, getting in the last word. Clearly satisfied his work was done, Deefur turned round and trotted back inside, finally as obedient as you like, to take his place in the pool of morning sunlight filling the kitchen, the remains of the cabbage between his huge paws. Cameron waited at the still-open door, in a daze. There went his last chance, the last suitable nanny on the Agency's list, a list that wasn't that long to start with. Emma buried her tears in his shoulder, her murmured "chocca" getting quieter and less *there,* to his intense relief. He closed the front door behind them, effectively closing them off from the world outside. He leaned against the door and slid down to sit, legs stretched in front of him and cradling his whimpering daughter in his arms.

Deefur remained quiet. The big, largely friendly giant took up most of Cam's tiled kitchen floor, and not for the first time in the past few months Cam's knifing resentment rose at the chaos in his house. He didn't mean to. He loved Deefur, he really did, and he didn't want to resent *Mark's* dog, but it was getting so damn hard not to. *Mark.* He had been the one to decide they needed to be a family, declaring a dog a good start. As much as Cameron tried, he couldn't forget the day they brought him home.

"Deefur dog," Mark had declared.

"Look at the size of his paws. He's gonna be huge. What about Hercules, or — I don't know — something for a big dog, like, we could be ironic, call the puppy Tiny or something?"

"Nope. Deefur is so much cooler," Mark responded cheerfully to what Cam knew was a blank expression, "D-for-Dog, get it?"

Cameron was in love enough to go with the flow. For both the mixed breed dog with the uncertain parentage — Great Dane and who knew what else — and the huge paws and the equally stupid name. In no time at all the puppy with the sticky-up ears, the melting chocolate eyes, and the irrepressible doggy grin had become an adult dog.

Still, with the eyes, he could worm his way out of many a bad situation with a single doleful look. Cameron loved dogs — he considered himself a dog person — but with his company growing so fast…

They were a victim of their own success, clients demanding more for less, and then the whole surrogacy thing had happened so damn

Deefur Dog

quickly; sometimes everything had been too much. They had muddled through though, Mark and Cameron, as they did with everything; with a lot of laughter, a few arguments, and one hell of a large amount of dog poo bags. Deefur became Mark's dog, and the damned idiot fur-frenzy absolutely adored the older man, following him everywhere, earning the nickname Shadow. Mark's shadow. Mark's dog.

"Maybe you should think about loaning Deefur out somewhere for a while?" his mom had suggested on her last visit. She had been picking cans, boxes, and other recycling items from the hedge where Deefur stored them for some weird purpose. "Just maybe until Emma goes to preschool?" Cam agreed at the time. She made one hell of a lot of sense. Yes, handling work and Emma would be easier if he didn't have to deal with Deefur too. But who the hell did you *lend* dogs to?

Deefur had literally become the one part of his life Cameron couldn't reconcile. Mark had been gone a long time now. Taken on a frigid January morning when black ice, soft snow and an oncoming semi meant Mark never made it home from an overnight trip. Eighteen long months — a year and a half — with Emma doubling in size and passing her second

RJ Scott

birthday, her long brown hair and blue eyes so much like Cameron's. There would never be one hint of Mark's wheat-blond hair or his beautiful, hazel green eyes. Eyes which constantly sparked with emotion and enthusiasm for life. Nope, she was only ever going to get Cameron's dark hair, his blue eyes, or maybe lighter brown hair like the birth mother, because Cameron's genes had been used in this surrogacy. The plan had been for Mark's turn to be next. Whatever obstacles they had to overcome, they were determined to have at least two children if they could. Mark worked from home, an accountant, the least boring accountant Cameron had ever met. He was there for the baby, for Emma... most of all he dealt with Deefur on a day to day basis, walked him, groomed him, trained him. His death left all three of them at a loss.

Cameron believed it was only luck that got him through each day so he could take care of Emma and meet her needs. Grief kept a bubble of isolation around them, but the biggest loser always would be Deefur. Cameron gave into everything he wanted and paid the dog enough attention for Deefur to remain healthy. Walked. Fed. Brushed. But when it came to discipline? Well, that became non-existent. Cameron had neither the time nor the inclination to worry. So

Deefur Dog

now Deefur ruled the damn house, and Cameron had no control in the slightest over the one-hundred and forty pound Great Dane cross. Walks involved Cameron being dragged down the street, pulled like a small kid on the leash. Peace in the house involved locking Deefur out in the yard, or in various rooms to keep him out of Emma's and his stuff. He was exuberant, playful, a big, overgrown, hairy puppy who single-handedly cleared a room with his over-excitement.

No, today had been the final straw. He couldn't deal with Deefur's behavior, and the dog reminded him too much of the man Cameron had married, the man he wanted to raise children with. He couldn't handle it. He couldn't. Not anymore. He struggled enough with the breath-consuming grief on his own, looking after a two-year-old daughter and a business partner who relied on him. Deefur needed a family with acres of land, people who had time, a family who was more than *just* scraping by on a day to day basis. When he weighed up the pros and cons in his head, the con column was about a foot long and no other choices remained. He wasn't capable of giving the high-spirited dog a good home anymore.

Deefur had to go.

Chapter 2

"I'm sorry, Mr Everson. We are fully aware of your skill set, but we don't have any matches."

Jason sat and listened, refusing to let the news get him down as he sat in the administration office of the Agency. Sitting here at the best of times with no hope of possible employment was hard enough. Added to this, he had to listen to his shortcomings being listed by the *officious official* who *officially* told him he was completely unemployable.

"I've said this before, young man. I'm sorry, but people don't always want male nannies. Especially young male nannies with little or no actual experience." Add the unspoken 'gay nanny', and there remained no job or even the slightest prospect of a job. The fact he had helped his momma raise his five younger brothers and sisters, plus his qualifications, criminal checks, and references didn't appear to matter one little bit.

"Anyway, Mr—erm," she checked her paperwork and he winced. Jeez, not even important enough to have his freaking surname recalled. "Everson. Surely it can't be long until

Deefur Dog

you graduate?" The helpful Agency owner had an enormous amount of optimism and expectation on her face. He imagined the forced smile was used to hide the relief the unemployable would be leaving their books soon.

"Another year. I only need something for the year. There must be—something?"

"Have you thought of advertising as a babysitter in the papers?"

"A babysitter?" Jason flinched inwardly, horrified at the word. His qualifications and experience put him way past odd nights here and there as a babysitter. Okay, so much of his experience leaned towards the informal, but he had been a nanny for the Mitchener's kids for four months and they loved him. Unfortunately, they had emigrated to Canada and had taken his position with them.

"I'm sorry. We have your details, and as soon as there is a suitable match..." Her voice trailed off and she glanced towards the door expectantly. Clearly his cue to leave, and with a singular disappointment knifing through him, he thanked her for her time and left.

Glass half full was how he looked at the world. A positive kind of person normally, the world around him consisted mostly of a sunny, happy, positive place, and generally he saw the good in everything. Today though, leaving the Agency office, two days before his twenty-fifth birthday, there was no good to see in an eviction notice, an empty bank account, and no job. The words of the Agency's dismissal ringed in his ears. Moodily he scuffed at the grass underfoot as he walked, realizing he had reached his shabby, barely-holding-it-together truck without even remembering the walk to get there. This was stupid. He needed to get a grip. After all, if everything went seriously wrong, if he had *really* run out of options, then he could always go home, back to his parents' house. The door remained open to him, always.

Other twenty-five-year-olds got help from their parents; he wouldn't be the first. His mom would jump at the chance to have her eldest child back at home, and for a moment, the prospect made his breath catch. Back to his family, his siblings, well, the ones still at home anyway, made a pang of self-pity curl in him. *This is silly. I'm not giving up now.* So close to passing the requisite teaching exams, so damn close; three terms remained, and there must be something he could do. A part-time job at Joe's Pizza Parlor filled most of his spare time with

Deefur Dog

minimum wage pay and pathetic tips. He had to find something paying well enough so he could leave the pizza job and concentrate on the final three terms. Otherwise, he may as well kiss his career hopes goodbye.

Always a late starter — Jason took a long time to decide what to do with his life and now, at the last hurdle, everything was going wrong. There were so many different paths he had tried to take; baseball-guy, advertising agency trainee-guy, writer-guy, all the time being pulled back to what instinct told him he would be good at: teaching kids. Not teenagers, but younger kids with their eyes full of wonder, little sponges thirsty for knowledge. His second brother Nathan had often said Jason appeared little more than a kid himself, anyway, which was why the kindergarten kids loved him so much. Said comment had caused the usual Everson pile-up with Nathan victorious — again — damn his extra weight and sneaky poking-in-the-eye maneuvers.

Thinking of his family left Jason feeling decidedly blue as he peeled out of the parking lot and found himself heading to Billy's on automatic pilot. Right then he couldn't think of anywhere else he wanted to be, and eventually he turned his old truck into the pot-holed staff parking and left it there. Then, not fit for human

RJ Scott

company, he bypassed the office and went straight to the dogs. There would be coffee and sympathy from Billy if he wanted, but at this point in time, he wanted to wallow in the unfairness of life. Always ready with coffee, Billy had a wealth of understanding and a wise word for any situation. Jason wasn't ready for someone being nice to him, not until he calmed down, allowing the total adoration and love of the rescued dogs to work their magic on him.

He found rare peace in his volunteering at the animal shelter and wished he had more time to offer his canine friends. Pulling down leashes, he started the daily cycle of dog walking. He scrambled and ran; enjoying the quiet acceptance of the rescued dogs. From Lacy the King Charles, to Bear the Husky, he walked them in the fields behind the sanctuary, while uncomfortable thoughts raced through his head. He anticipated the eviction notice on his rooms. The landlord had plans to remodel and sell up. Jason's money to live on had run low. He didn't earn enough for a deposit or monthly rental, and he had to keep some back for his college courses. He already juggled a part-time job with his studies and still had nowhere near enough money to cover everything.

Billy had said he could stay overnight in the

Deefur Dog

office if he got desperate, but he couldn't *employ* Jason. He didn't have the money. Jason wasn't stupid — the dog rescue didn't have excess funds to support *any* staff and relied on volunteers like him and donations of food and money. He had thanked Billy for the offer of the pull-out couch in the office as a last resort, his pride dictating he would rather end up sleeping in his ancient truck.

With a degree in child psychology and a teaching qualification as near as damn it in the bag, finding a position looking after kids should be easy. Maybe slightly easier if he hadn't been so honest about his sexuality during the informal first interview. Shit, why the hell he should hide? Being gay didn't make him some kind of sexual deviant. Frustrated by his thoughts, he slumped down next to the nursing pen. The Retriever dumped at Billy's last week lay on her side, panting with exhaustion and heat. She had been discarded pregnant and close to birthing. Now there were ten puppies crawling around her, searching for milk.

Instinctively Jason leaned over to help. He smiled down at the tiny blind creatures, guiding them to the source, lifting one tiny pup where two could fit in his palm, and he wished he could take one of them — two of them — all of them, to a home. His home. His *own* home. There was a peace in having a dog, a natural love you could only get from a dog, and he missed owning one.

Here with the animals, Jason didn't feel so helpless, or out of control. After allowing himself the ten minutes of self-pity he needed, he pulled off his t-shirt, wiping at the sweat on his face and neck, and moved back out into the sunshine to walk the next group of dogs. His mood lingered, but had lightened considerably, and for the perspective, he was grateful.

Deefur Dog

Chapter 3

Neal flew to Cameron's rescue, taking Emma for the day and carrying her off to the site with him. Their fledgling business teetered on the edge of being big and couldn't handle at least one of them not being on site. Neal rationalized it all for Cameron—made what Cam had to do easier.

"If Deefur has a new home, a big house, maybe with more space, owners at home all day, and then, without Deefur, you know it will probably be much easier to find help with Emma."

Cameron and Mark had split their time equally. Childcare had been an important thing for them, they both wanted to be hands-on parents. Now with it being Cameron on his own—it was damn hard. He had tried several local agencies by recommendation, nannies with impeccable references. All of them had bravely sat through the interviews, until the whole Deefur thing had been introduced, or his lifestyle came into the discussion, or his opinion on Emma's upbringing had been mentioned. Not one of them stayed longer than a week, and the

28

last one, well, that one quite clearly hadn't even made it through the door. Neal's advice made sense.

Which was why, on this hot Saturday, under a clear blue sky, Cameron sat in his truck with Deefur panting and drooling in the front seat next to him. He willed himself to get out of the cab and to actually go into the place his mom recommended.

Billy's Dog Rescue.

"The best place, Cam," Neal had agreed softly. "It has a good reputation, and they don't put the dogs down. It's this huge ranch-type place, and they re-home. They spend time finding the right families, the right owners — "

Cameron looked at Deefur, who stared back at him, his mouth wide in a doggy grin. His brown eyes were sparkling and excited by the journey in the truck, said journeys generally ending up in a walk of some description. In his mind's eye, Cameron saw Mark standing at the door, a bundle of sable fur in his arms and a huge bashful smile on his face. Full of ideas for walks and eager to buy puppy food, bedding and a crate. The same crate Deefur grew out of in three months, the same crate that still sat in the garage complete with bite marks and missing hinges; the

Deefur Dog

result of the great Deefur escape attempt of Christmas Eve.

"Don't look at me like that," Cameron said softly, burying his face in Deefur's soft fur, the smell of freshly shampooed dog in and around him, and the nuzzle of a cold, wet nose against his skin. He wanted a way to explain; to make this huge dog with a heart of gold understand why he needed him to go to a new home, why his very presence made Cameron's and Emma's lives so damn difficult. "I'm sorry," he murmured into the fur. Then he clipped the leash to the collar and opened the door, encouraging Deefur out and across the grass, which Deefur promptly scent-marked, and then spent time exploring on the long lead as Cameron locked up the truck.

Cameron stopped under the ranch-style sign and tugged on the leash. Deefur happily jumped ahead, his joy in the summer day in every sniff and whine as he discovered the grass and the dusty path. Finally Cameron stood at the door to the cabin-like office, with the words "Welcome Dogs and People" carved into old wood. With a determined straightening of his shoulders, he pushed open the door making an old-fashioned bell jingle. He hesitated only for a moment, the words, the reasons, and the excuses suddenly tumbling out of his mouth in a heated

RJ Scott

rush to the white haired man sitting behind the desk.

"I need you to take this dog his name is Deefur he is four, my daughter is two I have my own company he is too big, too big for us I can't handle him and I can't find a nanny to help with my daughter when he is there. He was my partner's dog but see he's — my partner — he passed away, and I'll pay his board until you find a home for him, a good home, but I need you to take him, so — please." Cameron hadn't even stopped to breathe or to even look at the person who stood patiently staring over the desk at Deefur.

"You wanna take a seat?" he asked and Cameron sat, quickly and suddenly. Every ounce of energy had left him. "Coffee?" asked the same gruff voice, and Cameron found himself saying *yes*; found himself looking out of the window at the kennels and dog runs behind the office, found himself drinking hot, almost-black coffee as the other man sat back down and listened. Finally finding himself telling this man, *this nodding, understanding man,* the whole problem from start to finish. The reasons why he sat here, even as he sat desperately holding onto Deefur's lead with his right hand, absently stroking the huge shaggy head with his left, coffee

Deefur Dog

abandoned, his knuckles white with the grip on the lead.

* * * *

Billy Pearson looked carefully at this man who sat clinging desperately to the long leather leash, this Cameron Jackson. He focused on the other man's left hand buried deep into his dog's fur, took in the dog's wet nose, the brushed coat, the clear eyes. Through narrowed eyes he read the body language, at the man's own eyes, suspiciously bright, and he made the decision there and then. With no hesitation on his part, Billy stood and opened the back door, the one marked *Staff* and shouted two words out into the dust beyond.

"Stretch, office!" He tapped his fingers, watched the man and refilled his coffee, offered a biscuit to Deefur, and glanced repeatedly out the window until finally he saw Jason jogging this way.

He wondered how much to tell Jason. Should he mention Cameron had a *male* ex-partner, or would he be seen as being some kind of matchmaker? He decided it might be better coming from this Cameron Jackson himself. He smiled as the office door flew open; Jason never did anything quietly. The young man's worn jeans were covered in mud, his t-shirt off and tucked in his belt, his chest bare to the sun, and his hair damp and plastered back on his head. He looked impossibly young and fresh from exercising the boarders, jumping up the final steps and banging in through the door. Billy smiled at his entrance.

"Wassup?" Jason smiled, dropping to fuss at the dog sitting in the middle of the office, crooning a hello, and then standing up to look at Billy and Cameron expectantly.

* * * *

Cameron sat dumbstruck, startled at the entry and at the young man who stood in the open doorway. The young *half-naked* man, the young half-naked, impossibly gorgeous, sweaty man with the muscles. Really tall, probably five or so inches taller than him and clearly not a stranger to the gym. Short, dark, sweat-damp hair clung flat on his head and his gaze skittered from dog to him, and then back to Billy. He pulled his t-shirt from his jeans to wipe his face, and in the time it took him to do that, Cameron

Deefur Dog

lost the power of rational speech.

"Jason, we got us a reject. This here's Deefur," Billy said firmly, crossing and taking the lead from Cameron and handing control over to the tall newcomer. Who switched from affable youth to pissed-off man in an instant.

"A reject? What is it?" Jason drawled, talking directly to the dog, scruffing the fur around Deefur's huge floppy ears. "Did he get tired of you now you're not a puppy?"

"I'm not—" Cameron started to splutter. That wasn't fair, but the new guy dismissed excuses.

"Whatever. It's nothing we can't handle," Jason snapped, guiding Deefur towards the exit door.

"Don't I get to—" *say goodbye?* Cameron wanted to say. He wanted to stop them, to grab back the lead. Deefur wasn't their dog yet, and as the owner he had rights—surely—

Jason turned back, waiting expectantly for Cameron to finish the sentence. When Cameron could think of nothing to say and the pause grew too long, Jason shrugged. With disappointment and anger carving his face, he opened the door and started to leave the office, Deefur following calmly.

"Wait—no—" Cameron said, standing and taking a single step towards his dog, "I didn't reject him—I can't—it isn't as simple as it seems—please—"

Jason, *tall guy*, stopped, a simple softening in his expression, as he waited, looking again between Billy and Cameron, clearly waiting for guidance.

"Jason," Billy began, "can you stay for a bit?"

* * * *

Cameron stood uneasily outside the office, his head still spinning. This sounded like a set up. Or too good to be true. To find someone who loved dogs and in a position to nanny, even temporarily for a year, added up to something way beyond his expectations.

"So, you're like a nearly qualified teacher? For real?" Cameron realized he probably sounded like he didn't believe him, "*and* you just happen to be in your last year at college, you like dogs, *and* you volunteer here?"

"Yes." Jason nodded, his own face marked with caution. Cameron knew it was too good to be true and actually anticipated a punch line of some sort.

Deefur Dog

"And you are looking for work?"

"I need something to help me finance my thesis, allowing me to study from home, and I'm looking for somewhere to live."

"Where are you living now?" Cameron didn't mean to sound so damn suspicious but hell, either luck had landed finally on his side or he'd become the target in one hell of a practical joke.

"My landlord is relocating and developing the place I rent to sell." Far too late Jason attempted to look like he didn't care. Cameron had already heard the disappointment in the other man's voice.

"You sure you could handle a two year old *and* a dog? A big dog, a Great Dane." Cameron emphasized the big dog part, his instantaneous reaction, and his immediate worry. Deefur had become such a handful. Then he felt guilty almost straight away. Emma. Could this half-naked guy actually be the right person to look after Emma? Shit. Half-naked. Cut. Clearly worked out, looked after himself. Emma… Focus on Emma… *Emma…*

Jason laughed, dropping to his knees next to Deefur, who instantly rolled on his back showing his belly for a rub. "Yeah, no worries, man."

"I would need references — for Emma — " Cameron said a little desperately.

"I have them." Jason answered simply. "I have all my police checks, and I am actually registered in town with the Adams Nanny Agency."

The Adams Agency? The same agency he had tasked to find him a nanny? Cameron wondered why the agency hadn't sent Jason out on an appointment for the position, but swiftly put the thought to the back of his head. Maybe the guy had a homophobic streak and the agency knew this? Perhaps he had specified he wouldn't work with a family once comprised of two dads. Should Cameron tell the prospective nanny about Mark now rather than later? No, he should leave it until he had more of a handle on this whole thing. He didn't have to offer this Jason a job today. He could check references, ask around, and make sure this six-three, tight-bodied man fit the job.

Cameron pressed fingers against the ache forming in his temple, wondering what the hell he could be thinking, trying not to look at delineated muscle-tone and sun kissed skin, or focus on spiky, dark brown hair and the hint of

Deefur Dog

dimples in a wide smile. He tried desperately to imagine how life could be easier if only he could find a nanny, and how this solution, this Jason guy, would mean he could hang on to the only link he had left to Mark.

Deefur.

Chapter 4

Jason eased back against the concrete wall of the pound, an old dog leaning into him and allowing himself to be brushed where he stood. Scribble's ancestry clearly held some poodle, maybe Labrador, definitely a hybrid of quite a few breeds apparently, but poodle fur predominated. He had been dropped off on Thursday by the landlord of a man who had died in the apartment block he owned. The man, in his eighties, had died of natural causes, the vet confirmed Scribble didn't have long to go either. Cancer being the primary diagnosis, but his kidneys were bad and his eyesight failing. A quiet dog, and nearly fourteen, his health was deteriorating rapidly and nothing Jason could do today was going to stop the inevitable. Scribble missed his owner. Jason wanted to spend time with the old boy, chatting to him about nothing while easing the stiff brush through tangled fur.

"You are looking fine," Jason reassured Scribble who simply looked up at him with sad eyes, his mouth open and his tongue lolling to one side as he panted in the heat. "We're gonna get you a girlfriend in no time…"

Deefur Dog

"How's he doing?"

Jason looked up, blinked into the bright light and focused on Billy, who stood outside the run of Scribble's cage area.

"He's doing good, aren't 'cha boy." Jason scratched behind Scribble's ears, and the old dog leaned more into the touch. Jason allowed Scribble to rest to one side so the canine's head lay in his lap. It was a comfortable position in which to sit and listen as Scribble's sighing became the steady, deep breathing associated with sleep. Neither he nor Billy were happy to lose a dog, even one as old as Scribble, and Billy looked content to sit with Jason and keep him company as they waited.

"So, you got an interview then?" Billy settled himself against the opposite wall and slid until he sat on the floor, smiling as Jack the black Lab wandered over and used him as a pillow. Jack had been placed at the center a long time ago, and for some reason, Billy never parted with him, and he became as much a part of the furniture as Billy.

"Yeah, wants to see me tomorrow. Probably won't get the contract though."

"'Course you will."

"Too good to be true, Billy —"

"You got the skills," the older man interrupted, "the experience. You like dogs. You're perfect."

"So why didn't the Agency send me before, if I am so perfect?" Scribble huffed in his sleep, his paws moving slightly. Jason smiled. He loved when dogs dreamed and imagined Scribble dreaming of a field somewhere with his owner, running and chasing a ball.

"Maybe it wasn't obvious you were perfect?"

"I'm a qualified, police-checked, experienced nanny, and I like dogs—tell me where it wasn't obvious? No, I know why they didn't match me. I should have told him everything I told the agency, full disclosure. Given him the chance to withdraw the offer of interview before it went this far."

"Told him?"

"About being gay."

"What bearing does orientation have on the situation?" Billy asked gently. Jason didn't look at the older man.

"I'm not clueless. Some people are still reluctant to deal with it, and the Agency said—"

"Ignore the Agency, boy, they don't know anything about you."

Deefur Dog

Jason wished he could believe what Billy said, but so far in six months of being on the books, he hadn't been offered one nanny position, and he was convinced his being gay was the reason why. God, why did he even tell them? If he'd kept his mouth shut, not let it go wandering ahead without his brain being in gear, then he would have a contract by now. They didn't even ask him. It wasn't on their list of questions, couldn't be on the list. No, he had blurted the whole thing out. Stupid, *stupid*.

"I don't want to have to go home," he said simply, "if this doesn't work out, then I can't see any alternative."

"They got a problem with you back at home, being gay 'n all?"

"No." Jason laughed. "God no. They would have me back in an instant." Wandering out of the closet had been damn easy. His family supported him, his friends didn't care, he had a bright shiny future, and he even had a boyfriend at school. He still had the future, although the boyfriend had fallen by the wayside. The future *he* wanted just wasn't falling in his lap. For the first time ever, he had reached an obstacle in his life he could attribute directly to being gay. "I need to stay here, get my qualifications, and then get myself a job."

They sat for a while discussing the dogs, the rescue center, the job, when Jason noticed his charge had stopped twitching and dreaming. He moved his hand from Scribble's furry ears to his frail chest to check for the rise and fall of breathing. He felt nothing and looked at Billy, who shuffled over to touch Scribble in the same manner.

"He's gone," Jason half whispered, emotion tight in his voice.

"Went to be with his daddy," Billy replied. "I'll go call the veterinarian."

Jason sat there for a long time, waiting for the vet to arrive, a whole multitude of emotions slipping through him. Sadness for Scribble. It didn't matter the poodle mix hadn't been here for long, Jason always got so attached to the dogs at Billy's. Added to that was worry for the interview, and fear. The fear constituted a new experience, but he identified the fear of failure sitting heavy in him.

He didn't want to admit how today had been the worst day of his adult life, but he was scared about the interview, scared to tell Cameron Jackson about being gay, and wondering if that single detail meant his prospective employer would tell him to get lost.

Deefur Dog

For the first time in his life, Jason wondered if he should hide his sexuality.

Chapter 5

Totally and utterly too good to be true. It had to be. The tall guy, Jason Everson from the dog home was scheduled to arrive in half an hour, and his résumé and references had arrived by fax to Cameron's home office at seven in the morning. There had been a curt covering note from the Adams Agency introducing Jason Everson, age twenty-five, and another reference from the local college. At first, Cameron had reservations about looking at the guy's grades. What kind of person was he to make assumptions about Jason — his life and habits — based on a string of A's, when he himself was only four years older and probably not much wiser? Then Cameron shook himself; he had a young daughter, and where Emma was concerned, he would check Jason's shoe size if he thought it would help keep her safe.

A hyper Emma jumped from toy to toy, to DVD to biscuits, demanding a drink, chattering nonsense, and climbing all over Deefur, who simply lay still and allowed Emma free rein. Cameron rubbed his chest, as if the action alone could still the ache in his heart. Seeing Emma with Deefur hurt so much. They had planned, he

Deefur Dog

and Mark, to extend the family, to give Emma a younger brother or sister. She shouldn't rely so much on Deefur, and grief so damn real, missing his husband and lover, hit Cameron like a hammer.

The hand of the clock clicked 'round another minute to Jason's arrival, and Emma apparently sensed his anxiety, or possibly made a lucky guess as to what her daddy needed.

"Dadda? Jay-an-an?" Emma asked softly as she climbed onto Cameron's lap. Cameron had spent a little while talking to her, more to hear the sound of his own voice in reassurance mode, about a possible nanny, a man called Jason, explaining how this Jason may be looking after her from today if Daddy thought Jason could be a good nanny. He added how Jason would be her friend, but she should mind him. She had listened, in the way two year olds had, easily distracted by purple dinosaurs and catchy music. Still, to hear the way she tried to say Jason, the missing 's', the extra 'an' on the end — sounded very cute.

"He'll be here after your nap, Pumpkin. Go get under the covers, and I'll be in there in a minute." She clambered down with no argument, and then scampered away, jumping over an accepting and half asleep dog. She was an angel in his life, a blessing, a beautiful, sparkly child lit from the inside by a pure heart. Mark had never seen his baby grown, never would, having only held her as a tiny newborn. Cameron's favorite image, and one he didn't have as a photo, just as a memory in his mind—Mark on the sofa in the sun room, sleeping, with Emma curled on his chest, her diapered bottom upright, her tiny fingers clinging to Mark's sleep shirt.

Cameron dropped to his knees beside Deefur. He couldn't even begin to remember things without triggering his barely concealed emotions. Instead, he began brushing Deefur's fur. The therapeutic action, sitting in the sunshine in his and Mark's kitchen, brushing at the sable softness, chuckling as Deefur rolled onto his back and tried to bite at the brush. This happened every day; every brush stroke accompanied by Deefur trying to stop the process with half-hearted nips and pulls, ending ultimately with movements too lazy to actually prevent the grooming but were still fun to try. Cameron couldn't believe he still had Deefur here in his house. He was putting an awful lot of faith in this Jason guy. A nanny who was the eldest of several siblings, and said he could handle Deefur as well. Cameron would believe it when he saw it.

Deefur Dog

Cameron lost himself in thoughts of what ifs, listening to Emma singing along to Barney, finally quiet as her morning nap caught up with her. What if this Jason could help him for real? What if he was good with kids and could control Deefur? Maybe, finally, Cameron would have some space to get his head sorted.

What if it didn't work? What if he really hated kids? Would Cameron be prepared to leave his baby girl with a stranger, a man he didn't really know, and shit—he was all for equality, but what if a male nanny was the worst decision he ever made? Deefur harrumphed and rolled over to sleep, and Cameron leaned against his warm body. He pulled his cell out of his pocket and pressed the pound sign for Neal, suddenly so desperate to get some perspective on this.

"Cam, he there yet?" Neal didn't bother with hellos; they didn't need to, having only spoken to each other half an hour earlier.

"Ten minutes and I'm scared shitless I'm doing the wrong thing."

"Because?"

"Because he's a grown man looking after my little girl?" Cameron allowed his fear to drip into his words.

"His references check out?"

"Uh huh."

"You told me he is a straight-A student at college?"

"Uh huh."

"He has experience?"

"Neal!"

"Jeez, Cameron, he's filling every single box with ticks, you have to trust someone."

"I don't know him, and if I give him the job, he'll be a live-in nanny. I've never done that before—what if he hurts Emma, or me, or shit—I don't know…"

Neal used his best, calm, brotherly voice, "So take off the next few days."

"It's just—none of the other nannies stayed during the night."

"You said you offered him a room because he had nowhere to live."

"It made sense when I said the words."

"And now?"

"I'm not ready to leave him with Emma." He stopped, knowing he didn't really need to vocalize his worries. Neal would know what he meant.

"Take the days, get to know him, see what is

49

Deefur Dog

what, work from home. I can cover the build."

Cameron didn't think he could love his brother more for simply knowing Cameron needed a few days to check Jason Everson out.

"I owe you one."

"You owe me loads; later." Neal rang off with a laugh, and Cameron, for the first time since yesterday, actually smiled.

* * * *

Jason stood outside the house, a large new build with a six-foot fence around the perimeter. The solid fence secured with a wrought iron gate. The guy at number fourteen, two doors down, stared at him; Jason could sense beady eyes boring into his neck, and he shifted his bags from one hand to the other before slipping the latch on the gate. He stepped into the grassed front yard, pulling the gate closed behind him, and then climbed the three steps to the front door. He looked back at his beat up truck parked on the curb, at the disapproving looks from the guy down the street, and squared his shoulders. Time to grow up, get a job, get some responsibility. Taking a deep breath, he knocked on the door and waited.

Cameron answered the door, looking as gorgeous as he did on Saturday, blue eyes, dark hair, and the slim build and the lashes—Jason swallowed and extended his hand, which Cameron took without hesitation, tugging gently and making Jason take the first steps into his potential new life.

"Please have a seat."

Jason sat on the very edge of the plain brown leather sofa, glancing around the living room empty of both dog and child and wondered if this constituted the first test. Perhaps any minute now Cameron would let both in just to see how Jason handled the situation. The very thought made Jason sit upright; he wasn't going to screw this up. Cameron sat in the seat opposite, pulling out a red file and flicking through papers. Silence grew, and his new employer lost himself in his thoughts.

"Where are Emma and Deefur?" Jason finally asked, more for something to say than for a response, but Cameron lifted his head, eyes unfocused. Was Cameron as nervous about this as Jason? Jason being Jason, simply did what he did best when he saw others in discomfort. He talked. "So. Go for it. Let's get all the awkward

Deefur Dog

questions out of the way," he said, and then he blushed, because really, he came across as slightly rude. Though Cameron did smile so that had to be a good start. Jason wriggled in his seat. He had thought long and hard about what he would say if Mr Jackson asked him outright about his sexuality. In his mind, he imagined standing up and demanding to know what right his prospective employer had to ask such a question. Then, in his mind, he saw himself go to pieces and almost beg for the job. This made for a lose-lose situation either way. What if he didn't tell Mr Jackson and he found out later? Would that be worse or better? Jeez, this was impossible. His rambling concerns were interrupted when the interview started, not with a question, but a statement from the man opposite. The cool, calm man who tapped the paperwork from the agency with his finger.

"I see you didn't go through the nanny screening in full or take them up on their available courses," Cameron said, poking at the form with his forefinger.

"No. None."

"I must admit I am used to the nannies I interview having undertaken every course from *Psychology of Bed Wetting* to *The Perfect Way to Puree* to *The ABCs of Poop*."

52

Jason's mouth dropped open. Was the man making a joke? He was certainly half-smiling, which implied his trying to lighten the tone.

"Can I be honest with you?" Jason knew this needed to be said and he didn't even give Cameron a chance to say yes or no. "They didn't like me at the agency, and I did try the puree course, but it was three hours of mashing carrots and networking. It really wasn't me."

"I can imagine," Cameron looked horrified at the thought.

"I never became a part of the wider nanny network there, and I didn't immediately fit the criteria they tick in their boxes. For one, I'm a man which put me firmly in the minority."

"Not a lot of men are nannies, I guess," Cameron offered with a nod. Jason exhaled a deep breath, fear of confrontation snapping at him inside. This was so freaking stupid, he should just say it. What harm could it do? He would rather avoid trouble down the line and deal with the fallout now before they went any further.

"For another thing—"

"Go on," Cameron encouraged with the same half smile.

"I'm gay." Jason kept the statement simple

Deefur Dog

and Cameron just stared at him. Although an unnerving reaction, at least Cameron hadn't leapt up and dragged Jason to the door.

"Okay," Cameron said finally, and Jason's stomach churned. What did Cameron mean "okay?" Possibly, "okay Jason, now leave"? Or, "okay I am cool with it"? Maybe even, "okay I am calling the cops"?

"I totally understand if my... erm... if it is a problem for you," Jason said, holding his hands in front of him in a gesture of peace, "but I just wanted to let you know, felt you should know up front. So if it is a deal breaker, you at least have the chance to be honest and tell me now so we're not wasting time for either of us."

Cameron blinked and Jason felt disappointment coursing through him. This had been too good to be true.

"Gay?" Cameron mumbled, all he could apparently manage to push out, clearly trying to process everything Jason had pushed at him in his rambling speech. Cameron said nothing else, simply stared, and Jason began to get more than a little bit uncomfortable.

He stood, pushing hands deep in his jeans pockets, trying not to show his burgeoning disappointment, and then crossed to the door.

RJ Scott

This may well have been the perfect job on paper, but he refused to have his sexuality define his life. He *would* be a kindergarten teacher, he *would* have a career, he didn't eat small children for breakfast, and he *would* leave this interview with his dignity intact.

"Thank you, Mr Jackson, for taking the time to see me," Jason said softly, his hand on the door handle.

"Wait," Cameron said, standing abruptly. Jason turned, readying himself for comments. Cameron picked up a photo frame, a simple stainless steel frame with a picture of a smiling man inside, a small babe in arms, and what appeared to be a younger Deefur to one side. "This is Mark. My partner for seven, God, nearly eight years. We met in college." Cameron paused, closing his eyes and shaking his head, momentarily silent. Jason wondered if he should say something, but he couldn't find the right words. "An accountant, a good one actually, totally the other half of me. He died almost eighteen months ago in an accident on the highway."

"Mr Jackson—" Jason desperately tried to find words to counteract the open grief in Cameron's eyes. Maybe he should focus on handling grief and not so much on the whole *I'm*

55

Deefur Dog

gay too thing, but Cameron interrupted, snapping back to reality in an instant.

"Cameron, call me Cameron, please," he said simply.

"Cameron then. I'm sorry for your loss," Jason finally said. Cameron simply nodded a quiet *'thank you'*.

"So you see," he continued, "our family — my family is kind of unconventional, and matched with Deefur, it's scared all but one nanny away after a few days."

"One of the nannies stayed? Where is she now?"

"No, she never actually started. We never even got around to talking to the last one. She ran as soon as Deefur started barking. I have never seen a Toyota move so fast." Cameron sat down and half smiled, placing the folder back on the side. "I have other questions, but they can wait, and we can cover them at a later time."

Jason didn't want to get his hopes up, but Cameron sounded more positive than Jason expected he would.

"Okay." Words failed him. *Typical.* Jason *never at a loss for words* Everson, unable to string together a coherent sentence.

"So," Cameron paused, and then ticked off

items with his fingers, "Sundays off in full and alternate Saturdays, and living in. Living in is a new one for us, our nannies all lived locally and went home, so this is going to be a learning curve. Also we have this neighbor at number fourteen, Albert Caruthers, the wrong side of eighty. He isn't totally happy with me living here, being gay and all. Just ignore him if he corners you."

"Okay."

"You will, of course, have your own space. I need to get Neal over tomorrow to section off the third bedroom. I need his help with the dry-walling so we can hang a door, and then you, your bedroom and a half-bath, will be good to go."

"My own bathroom?" A step up from his rented rooms then. Back there he had shared a bathroom with the stinky, half-naked nameless guy in number twelve and Mrs Petunia Elvira Almond from down the hall, not a day under seventy.

"I have detailed a typical day for Emma; she is at a preschool club two mornings a week and I have also added in Deefur's routine, what there is of it." The last part Cameron added ruefully, clearly acknowledging Deefur didn't really have

Deefur Dog

a routine. "I want you to know, my time with Emma is precious, so I guess when I am here with her, you don't have to be around. It makes sense to use that as your time to study."

Jason nodded. As long as he had a desk in his room, he had peace and time to study.

"So, last thing I need to mention, I guess — Emma is genetically my child, we had a surrogate. Mark — " he stopped and took a deep breath, Jason could see the other man's grief. "We had plans for Emma, ideas of how we wanted, as gay parents, to raise her. I don't want her parents being gay pushed into her life; when it happens it will happen naturally. So, can I trust you will keep your relationships away from here, and not bring your lifestyle — men — boyfriends — to the house — until we get settled?" Cameron's seriousness made Jason think back to his last relationship some ten months ago, and the barren place his love life resembled since.

"No problem," he finally said. "I'll keep all my relationships away from here." Why the hell did he phrase it that way? He sounded like he had a million guys on the go at a time. He winced at his stupidity. Cameron didn't look fazed at first, but his smile did slip a little and there appeared to be a blush high on his cheeks.

"Okay — Emma is napping," Cameron looked pointedly at his watch, the frown of a clock-watching father on his face. "She needs another ten minutes then I'll go wake her up. So, Deefur first, I guess?"

"Where is he?" Jason followed Cameron down the corridor to a thick wooden door, hearing soft, snuffly, snorting behind the barrier, punctuated by low whines, and the odd *oofff*. Bracing himself for the onslaught, he waited as Cameron pulled open the door. In the flurry of sable and tail and paws, Jason got on his knees, his face and hands buried in long fur, murmuring sweet nothings into Deefur's ear. Deefur started to jump, and Jason pushed him down with a stern *no*, which Deefur obeyed with a quick thump of tail and an accompanying whine.

* * * *

Cameron watched as Jason got down and dirty with the dog, first on his knees, and then with firm commands, muscles bunching and releasing under his t-shirt. Cameron stopped the twisting in his stomach with a sharp word to his libido. Just because the younger man announced

Deefur Dog

he was gay, didn't mean he would — and any stirrings of *God jeez hot* — well, they could stay where they were, because Jason as good as admitted he had a boyfriend, boyfriends, relationships — and shit, it hadn't even been long since Mark had died. He needed to get hold of his thoughts.

"Shall we get Emma?" he finally said, trying not to smile at how Deefur followed Jason as close as a shadow and led the way to the nursery and a sleeping Emma.

When they reached Emma's room, she still slept, curled in a tight ball under her quilt, her breathing even and deep. She looked adorable, long, straight, dark brown hair fanned out over the pillow, and her eyelashes rested on apple-round cheeks.

"She's beautiful," Jason whispered.

"She's a little angel," Cam replied, a flush of pride rushing through him, and leaned over her to kiss and tickle her awake. She climbed into his arms and peeked over his shoulder at Jason.

"Are you Jaynanan?"

"I am. You can call me J if you like."

"M'kay J. Daddy wan' down."

Cameron patted her diapered bottom, "We need to change your trainers," he said seriously, carrying her to a table and sitting her on the edge. "You want potty?"

"Nu huh," she replied, grabbing a handful of Cameron's shirt.

"You wanna do this yourself, Pumpkin?"

She nodded, scrambling down from the counter, using Cameron as a climbing frame, and scampered into the bathroom, half shutting the door.

"You said she's two."

"Two in May, so a little over two."

"And she's potty-trained?"

"Not really trained, but she doesn't wear diapers as such, just these training-pants things." He waved at the tumbling pile of trainer pants to the left of the small closet, and then added, "She wants to be grown up and change into her own new trainers sometimes."

"Independence is never a bad thing."

Emma emerged from the bathroom, lifting her arms and demanding to be picked up, Cameron obliged, patting her bottom again and hugging her approvingly.

"Shall we go visit with J and get some hot chocolate?"

Deefur Dog

Chapter 6

Cameron watched Jason with his daughter. Trying to be subtle about it, over the last two weeks he had been coming home early, leaving a little later in the morning, popping back at lunchtime for forgotten paperwork. If Jason cottoned on, then he never let on, and Cameron only ever saw happiness in his daughter and calm and peace in Deefur.

"I want to take Deefur to training. How do you feel about that?"

Cameron finished the mouthful of cereal. "Does he really need training lessons? You have him so in control."

"Dog companionship," Jason said, returning his attention to Emma who attempted to make a pasta collage under his direction. He righted a pot of glue and Cameron felt this overwhelming sense of relief at how easy it had become for Emma and him to have Jason in the house with them. Emma climbed down to go to the bedroom for crayons and Jason started to scoop up stray pasta, pushing aside a large board-backed book entitled *Play for Children Under Five*.

"Dogs need companions?" Cameron posed

62

RJ Scott

it as a valid question, but in reality he didn't want the conversation with his nanny to end as it meant he had to leave to go back to work, so he picked the first subject he could think of.

"Deefur can be a little —" Jason waved his free hand in what Cameron assumed was a gesture of *out there*. "He needs to socialize and start to learn it isn't appropriate to hump Mrs Smith's Chihuahua, or indeed, pee on her head."

"Mrs Smith?"

"The Chihuahua, Missy-Lulu-Bettany or something flowery. To be fair, Deefur didn't see her. He was marking and she was standing under him."

Hysterical laughter bubbled up inside Cameron and burst out of his mouth. Jason looked at him with an expression combining a smile and wry appreciation for the joke.

"Deefur — peed on Missy-Lulu-Bettany?" Sentences refused to form between laughter, but Cameron had clearly made himself understood when Jason started to join in. The two men laughed so loud Deefur started a whining accompaniment and only stopped when Cameron's flailing hand knocked the glue to the floor.

They both reached for the bottle, Jason

Deefur Dog

beating him by seconds, their hands brushing as Cameron pulled back.

"Sorry," Cameron offered softly.

"This glue is solid, anyway. We need more." Jason placed the glue back on the table and helped Emma back into her seat.

"I gotta go, Pumpkin," Cameron leaned in for a sticky-glue kiss and received some dried pasta.

"For eatin', Daddy," she said, and then smiled impishly when Cameron carefully placed the pasta in his top pocket.

"Beef stew okay tonight? I have this recipe my mom emailed me that I could use the meat in the freezer for," Jason asked and Cameron immediately replied.

"Cooking for us isn't part of your contract." It was the third time he had said that about the cooking, since Jason had presented lasagna and salad on Monday and pot roast on Tuesday. This would be the third night in a row.

"I enjoy the cooking, and Emma helps me. It's fun. As long as it's okay with you?" came the same response from Jason. Maybe they should end this apology/question thing with some direct talking.

"Jason, I would love if you cooked every

night, but if you do, I reserve the right to add a clause to your contract and pay you."

"I—" Jason looked ready to argue, and then clearly decided not to, subsiding into silence with a nod.

"I'll make sure you know when I am going to be home, then."

"Cool."

"Six tonight. We're on a local project." He leaned down to steal another kiss, and Emma patted the pocket containing the pasta.

"Bye, Dadda," she said, and then returned to the gluing project in hand, her tongue poking out of the side of her mouth as she concentrated.

They painted a serene scene, Jason comfortable with the glue and the pasta, Deefur asleep on the tiles, Emma so happy she was near busting with smiles. Perfect.

Cam wished he could stop waiting for it to all end.

* * * *

"Do you know where the leash is?" Jason called up to him, over the sound of happy whining and woofing. The fluster and

Deefur Dog

organization of a family outing for Father's Day didn't seem so cliché when Jason was involved. Cameron had packed a picnic lunch, trainer pants, wipes, snacks, water, sun cream, sun glasses, Emma's sunhat, and at last their little family appeared ready to move out.

Cameron came up with the idea, their first real weekend where he didn't have to work, and he wanted to walk the lake path, have a picnic, and watch Emma on the swings and slides. When he mentioned this to Jason, he casually asked the man if he would possibly be free on Saturday. He didn't even want to start analyzing the lightness in his heart when Jason said yes, that he loved the idea of a picnic. Nor did he want to begin questioning why he wanted to share Father's day with the nanny as well as his daughter. It couldn't be more than the fact that Cam simply enjoyed Jason's company. Jason was clever and quick, and funny, and kind of shy, and then not shy, and all kinds of things Cameron liked in a friend. Unspoken in his head were the added things he liked in a man, in a boyfriend, in a lover. Jason's height, the breadth of his shoulders, his broad chest, and the unconscious grace with which he dealt with anything thrown at him.

The day had started with breakfast in bed

and Cam pretending to be shocked an surprised at the toast slathered with peanut butter and the steaming coffee in his 'best dad' mug. Jason hovered at the door after helping Emma with the coffee to Cam's bedside table and then with a grin left the two of them. Cameron was ceremoniously presented with a pasta picture, and after thanking Emma the two settled back for a morning cuddle.

"I love you Daddy," Emma murmured, all morning warm and smelling of talc, he hugged her close.

"I love you too pumpkin."

And now, with leash found and Deefur in the back of the SUV, they set off for the lake, a gorgeous place holding so many memories. Jason sat in the seat next to him, and there was a palpable air of excitement as Emma babbled away in the back seat, commenting on trees, cats, other cars, and just how much daddy had loved the pasta picture. Cameron had become adept at translating the words, and Jason, in the short time he had been nanny, had become as experienced in Emma-ese.

The place they were going held so many memories for Cameron. Mark had carried Emma as a baby in a backpack arrangement when they

Deefur Dog

hiked the seven miles of pathways encircling the blue waters. This time Cameron brought a stroller, Emma now too big to carry but too small to walk all the way around the circle.

The parking lot was half full, but once they had walked away from the car and out onto the path, they were practically alone in the vast acreage of grass and trees.

"This place is beautiful," Jason observed, "I've never been here before."

"I haven't for a long time. The last time had been with Mark, when Emma was a baby. The weekend before the accident..." Cameron didn't want to finish the sentence, but Jason picked up on the reason and didn't push.

"Has it changed much?"

Cam swallowed his rising grief, grateful that Jason had changed the subject. "The parking area for cars is bigger, and I don't ever remember there being a concession stand," Cameron flexed his hands on the handles of the stroller, peering over to check on Emma, still sleepy from her half-nap on the journey here.

"Is she okay?"

"She's fine. She'll wake up with a vengeance in a minute, demanding all sorts of stuff. Drink, and chips and chocca."

"A sweet tooth just like her daddy." Jason stopped walking as Deefur pulled the lead to sniff at an area of trampled grass. Cameron stilled at the words. Mark had always commented on Cam's sweet tooth, in fact, if they ever argued, chocolate or candy could buy Mark back into Cameron's good books. Mark was so much on his mind today, and for good reason. His husband's birthday, which always fell one or two days away from Father's Day, was in a few days and yet another change of age Mark would never see.

"Mark always said…" his voice trailed off. He wanted to share memories with Jason, wondering if it was appropriate, but at the same time knowing he would share with a friend, and he considered Jason a friend.

"What?"

"That I had a sweet tooth."

"Dadda." The demand for attention came loud in the quiet of the air, and Cameron unstrapped her. Between her mission to totter on the edge of the water and Deefur's attempts to go swimming, no time remained for talking between the men, much to Cameron's relief. Suddenly he wanted memories of Mark to himself and didn't want to spend time dissecting and analyzing.

Deefur Dog

They stopped to eat at a point about ten minutes from finishing the walk, climbing a little up on a hill and spreading the thin blanket. The walk had been a long one, and when Emma had eaten her chips and sandwich and had drunk way more fruit juice than normal, she dozed off in the shade of a spreading oak, her thumb very firmly in her mouth.

"She shouldn't do the whole sucking thumb thing, should she?" Cameron remembered reading horror stories of deformed mouths and sticking-out teeth in toddlers who sucked their thumbs.

"Sucking your thumb when you are this little won't hurt, Cameron, I promise you she'll grow out of it when she needs to, or we'll help her to."

"I don't want her to have a deformed mouth or something."

Jason snorted at the words. "She will have a very beautiful mouth, soft, a bit pouty, full…" His voice had dropped a level and Cameron looked at him, startled to find him mere inches away as he reached into the basket for more water. He stared at Jason, who made no move to sit back down on the blanket. "She'll have lips like yours," he ended huskily, his gaze dropping

RJ Scott

to check out said lips, and Cameron's stomach clenched with the effort of not getting a freaking hard-on for the nanny.

"Lips… like mine?" Jeez Cam, you idiot, you did not just say that. Shut this conversation down. Now!

Jason leaned a little further, until only a breath separated them.

"Soft, kissable lips," he murmured so low Cameron almost couldn't make out the words, and then Jason did exactly what Cameron wanted him to do and placed the softest, most inquisitive of kisses on the lips he had waxed lyrical over.

The gentle kiss contained nothing more than an exchange of pressure, and then with a half groan Jason pressed for more, his hand sliding up to caress Cameron's face and his tongue gently touching Cameron's lower lip, asking for entrance. Cameron heard his own groan, parting his lips and deepening the kiss, and for long minutes kissing and tasting was all they did. Cameron didn't move his hands. Jason remained leaning over him with the one hand cupping his face. And then suddenly, completely, Cameron's head caught up with his dick. Scrambling back on the blanket, he placed a

Deefur Dog

finger to his damp lips. What the hell did he just do? He couldn't say a word, couldn't find the words to summarize the horror inside. Here, at his and Mark's special place, with his daughter not two feet away, he had compromised his freaking nanny, for God's sake.

Pushing the kiss to one side, he grabbed at items, forcing them roughly into the backpack, gesturing for Jason to move, and then throwing the blanket in the small basket under the stroller. Jason didn't say anything either. He simply walked in silence beside Cameron as they headed back to the car.

Jason, however, broke the awkward silence, a distraught expression on his face. "I'm sorry," the words were wrong spilling from his nanny's mouth.

"You're sorry?" How can it be Jason's fault? "I'm the freaking boss, I took advantage of you."

"You didn't—"

"I should be sorry, and I am. This won't happen again." He cut dead anything Jason may say with a single, rough hand movement. He didn't want to talk anymore. He climbed in the SUV and turned on the radio, 567 KTXM an easy cover for the silence.

They arrived home and Cameron didn't

know what to do next.

"I need to study," Jason stated and disappeared to his room. He didn't appear pissed, nor angry enough to leave the house, leave the home he was making for Cam's little family. *Shit,* he thought, *what the hell have I done? It would break Emma's heart to lose Jason. God, what if Jason left?*

Deefur Dog

Chapter 7

"How much yogurt did you manage to get down your top?" Jason teased, poking his pinky finger at Emma's ticklish tummy, causing her to collapse in a fit of giggles on the carpet in front of the TV.

"Lots and lots, J," she smirked, the dimples in her cheeks and the sparkling in her blue eyes, so close to his memories of Cameron's laughing over Deefur peeing on Missy-Lulu-Bettany's head.

"What is your daddy gonna say, Pumpkin?" he added, laying down next to her and rolling onto his back, Emma immediately taking the advantage and climbing on his stomach, using it as a mini trampoline.

"I love you, Pwincess." Emma offered, laughing between bounces, and Jason nodded, imagining exactly what Cameron would say, but still, teasing didn't hurt.

Three weeks had passed since the kiss. Three weeks of back-to-normal routine, Emma loved her J, Jason loved Emma, and as for Deefur, well, he appeared calmer, more in control of his huge paws and his hard, waggy tail, less oofy and pushy, more cute and docile. He had even formed an attachment to Missy-Lulu-Bettany that defied the odds, and not for the first time, Jason sent thanks to the veterinary gods that Cameron and Mark had sorted out having Deefur neutered. The physics of Deefur and Missy-Lulu-Bettany was something he didn't want to have to imagine. Jason hardly left the house for his own social life, even on his Sundays and alternate Saturdays off, and Cameron hadn't commented up to now. If Jason continued sharing evening meals when Cameron came in, Cameron didn't argue, and if Cameron and Jason ever became a distinct possibility after the heat of the kiss at the lake, then neither of them raised the subject.

There were sparks. Jason believed the attraction wasn't one-sided, but neither acted on the appeal, nor pushed for anything. Jason didn't expect anything, and for a long time the whole denial thing worked well.

"Hey, guys." Cam walked in, sleeves rolled up his arms, tie loose around his neck. He had been in zoning meetings all day and Jason knew how much his employer hated them.

"Daddaaa!" Emma pushed herself up and away from Jason's stomach and launched herself at Cam, who swung her high. Exchanging smiles

Deefur Dog

was enough for Jason to see how tired Cam was, and saying nothing Jason moved into the kitchen to finish making their dinner.

Dinner was fairly quiet, Cam clearly tired, Emma nodding off in her potatoes and Jason wondering how to word the question he had in his mind to ask. Cam cleared the table, Jason loaded the dishwasher and Cam carried the now sleeping Emma to her bed. He was gone for twenty minutes or so, enough time to brew fresh coffee and tidy up the rest of the kitchen. When Cam came back, he sipped coffee from his 'Best Dad' mug and then settled at the table with paperwork spread around him. Really it was now or never for the question.

"If it's okay with you, I want to volunteer for the local in-school reading program." Jason said, trying to mask his nervousness and the disabling sense it gave him. Cameron lifted his gaze from the papers he was poring over and blinked at the statement. Jason wondered if he had even heard. "I would be visiting the school both mornings that Emma is there."

"Okay, yeah, cool, good idea." Cameron was distracted, his mind clearly elsewhere, but Jason took his words at face value and decided to sign up the next day. On a few occasions at the school he had let slip to the Principal, who adored him, he was near as damn qualified to teach. It was a lovely school, not too big, in a district with surplus funds, and a Principal who loved the kids. The school had a Special Needs Department attached and, after dropping Emma to her preschool club, Jason had begun spending more time at the school assisting with a boy with mild autism and another who had Downs. This kind of rewarding work with all of the kids made him realize he had picked the right choice to become a teacher, and he guessed joining the reading program was a step in the right direction.

He looked to a future in this suburb of Tacoma; wanted to put down roots, to stay with the Jackson family, to teach at the local school, and on his more fanciful days, he wanted it to be forever.

* * * *

The loud and determined knock on the door made Jason hurry to answer before Emma woke up. To his surprise it was the neighbor who made a point of standing in his front garden and passing judgment on everything from parking issues to dog-mess. So far Jason had avoided him with a cunning use of hiding behind bushes until

Deefur Dog

the neighbor went indoors. This was after he spotted the unfortunate Mrs Smith and Missy-Lulu-Bettany being trapped between the unnamed neighbor and her car when she deigned to park a little over the marked line on the street.

"Is Mr Jackson here?" The little man asked, his moustache almost quivering with something like indignation across his thin upper lip, his beady brown eyes flashing with temper. Jason looked past him and to the front yard beyond, expecting something weird to be happening around the Terrier of a man. Jason's car looked to be parked correctly, and as far as Jason knew, he had picked up all the dog-mess he ever saw Deefur produce.

"Erm... Cameron is at work at the moment."

"Most inconvenient. Your dog," he spat the word "dog" out with venom, which made Jason think maybe Deefur had killed someone, "your dog has dug up every single rose in my yard."

"Deefur?" Jason glanced over his shoulder at the sleeping mound of fur who hadn't even deigned to move when the knock came on the door. He hadn't been out of Jason's sight all morning, and his paws were clean. "I don't think so, Mr... er..."

78

"Caruthers. And I will thank you to know I have evidence your dog was in my yard." Triumphantly, he held up a blue bag which looked suspiciously like a dog-mess bag, filled with what could Jason really hoped wasn't a big pile of poo.

"Evidence?" Jason searched for words. Mr Caruthers, number fourteen, twitching moustache and all and swinging a bag of dog poo at him as evidence that Deefur had committed some crime. "Sorry, but do you want to start from the beginning?"

"Your. Dog. Dug. Up. My. Yard." Mr Caruthers sounded out each word as if Jason were stupid. Jason could feel his anger build at the patronizing tone, but his polite nature forced him to hear the man out.

"When?" he asked as civilly as he could manage.

"This. Morning." Okay, still with the idiot explanation level.

"Aah, well, Deefur has been here the whole time. It couldn't have been him."

"I expected that from you. You and that man."

"I'm sorry?" Jason said, confused. Was the neighbor explicitly saying Jason was lying? And

Deefur Dog

what man was he talking about? Did he mean Cameron?

"Your kind. You come here," Little Man poked at Jason's chest, stepping over the threshold, "to a normal street, with your deviant ways, your kids and your dogs, set up home—" He went on and on, words of venom dripping from his mouth, every word punctuated by a stab of his fingers, the bag swinging dangerously close. The words spilling from his mouth were like nothing Jason had ever heard before. He went into shock. He didn't know what to say.

But that was okay because Deefur did it for him.

In a blur of fur and snarling, Deefur reacted to the poking and the prodding from the neighbor, and probably the fact said neighbor had crossed into the hallway. In seconds Little Man lay on his back, Deefur pinning him and snarling in his face. Jason, to his dying day, would swear black and blue that he pulled Deefur off immediately, but his conscience would likely tell him he actually left it a good ten seconds.

He tried not to laugh as Little Man scrambled free and ran for his life across the front yard, and out of the gate, pulling it closed behind him.

He disappeared off down the road, his arms flailing and his combed-over hair flapping. Jason looked down at Deefur who sat patiently at his side, a doggy grin on his snout.

Gently he patted him. "Good boy, Deefur, good boy."

When he recounted the tale to Cameron, who went from wide-eyed horror, to astonishment, to anger, and finally to a wry smile, Jason realized he was still in shock and poured a stiff whisky to settle himself. He had never experience hatred like that, but Cam seemed to be shrugging the whole thing off. He couldn't understand the calm reaction.

When Emma had gone to bed, he sat curled in his corner of the sofa blindly watching TV, thanking Cameron as he brought in coffee. To his surprise Cameron didn't take his usual chair, instead he sat next to him on the sofa and leaned into him, knocking shoulders.

"First time, eh?"

"First time?" Jason tried to make sense of Cameron leaning against him, but it proved hard to concentrate, let alone understand what Cameron was saying to him.

"For so much hatred and bigotry to happen

Deefur Dog

right in your face," Cameron offered softly.

"Yeah… I guess it is."

"It'll be okay." Cameron didn't say to ignore the hatred, or to forget it. He acknowledged it and simply offered support.

"It's happened to you a lot?"

"When I got married."

Cameron didn't elaborate and Jason didn't push. Cameron being next to him was enough.

He could grow to like this.

* * * *

Cameron came home late the following night. He had called ahead, apologized profusely, finally arriving home way past Emma's bedtime, to dim lighting and a snoozing Jason, six foot three inches of man sprawled this way and that on the main couch. For a few minutes he stood and watched, and wondered.

Something about Jason sent warmth to the pit of Cam's belly, and he wasn't entirely sure what it was. Maybe the way he helped Emma, the way he obviously loved Emma in particular and kids in general, perhaps how he controlled Deefur, his very presence calming the dog in seconds. Whatever magic Jason did in this house, Cameron loved him for it.

Loosening his tie, he slumped into the chair opposite the dozing nanny.

Jason woke up and blinked sleepily at him. "Hey," he said softly, glancing up at the clock "S'nearly midnight. You okay?"

"Yeah, m'okay, had a wiring failure and the contractors were late on site," Cameron said, laying his head back and sighing.

"Emma wants you to go give her a kiss." Jason yawned widely and stretched. Cameron just stared, taking his fill, focusing on the strip of warm skin showing as Jason's shirt rode up. This gorgeous man alone on a couch was a complete waste. Jason should have someone to share his life with. He was a good man. "We had a visit from a cop, said a local had informed him about a possible dangerous dog."

"Caruthers."

"I guessed so. Cop took one look at Deefur, asked a few questions, and then filed it away."

"Sorry you had to deal with it."

"It was fine. The cop was kind of hot." Jason raised his eyebrows and leered.

Cameron hesitated, questions on the tip of his tongue, wondering how to phrase his next

Deefur Dog

question and decided to be blunt.

"Why don't you ever go on dates?" He blurted out, and instantly regretted the move as Jason's eyes widened and he looked strangely at Cameron. "Because you can, you know… go out I mean… with men." Jeez, he sounded like a complete idiot.

"I know I can." Jason shifted to rest his elbows on his knees, his chin on his hands. "I don't want to date some random guy, and you don't exactly meet a load of gay guys at the school gate."

"See that's it—you never spend time away from us." This wasn't coming out right. He sounded like he had an issue with Jason never going out on dates, when in reality it was the farthest thing from his mind.

"Is it a problem? I could go out if you need the house, meet friends from the school, or from college. I can easily find somewhere else to—"

"No—there's not a problem—I… Look I don't want you missing out on *your* life because you are here making *my* life easier."

"I have a roof over my head, a kid I love like my own, a dog, and a friend in you. What else do I need?" Jason stood with another stretch, clearly ending the conversation. "'Night…"

84

RJ Scott

Cameron waited until Jason had left before collapsing back tiredly into the chair. He extended his legs and wished he had handled the whole question a little better. He meant to make Jason feel at ease, give the younger man the push to have time away from the house. He never meant to make him uncomfortable. So why, when his head fed him the words to say, didn't his heart want him to say a word?

Deefur Dog

Chapter 8

Neal loved Jason. He was as pleased to have Cameron back in the company at almost full capacity as he was glad to see his brother and niece happy and settled. They had a new contract starting on Monday, very hands on, no team this time, custom modeling on a brand new kitchen and breakfast room. Today, Sunday, they sat at the dining table, discussing project timetables and costs in the fall sunlight.

Cameron clearly didn't see anything wrong with the picture, nothing out of the ordinary, but Neal noticed. His eyes trained on activity outside the window, where Jason sat cross-legged looking at instructions and holding two pieces of brightly colored plastic. He bit his lower lip between his teeth and Emma sat by his side, an equally intense expression on her face. The scene looked very domestic, and a sudden worry hit Neal.

"Is Jason employed to work Sundays?" he asked suddenly.

"No, he has Sundays off," Cameron replied vaguely, his thoughts still focused on the work they were scheduling.

"Then why is he here today?" Neal finally said.

"Wanted to build the cube thing." Cameron mumbled, flicking sheets of paper and penciling a comment on sheet three.

"The cube thing." Neal sounded confused, apprehension growing inside him.

"Yeah, same as they have in preschool. Jason got it at a sale and said he'd build it." Cameron looked up with an irritable expression at not being able to concentrate. "It's a — " he waved his free hand expansively around his head, "cubey-climby thing."

"Cameron."

"Neal."

"I don't want to know about the cube thing. I want to know why your employee is here on his day off playing with Emma in your garden."

Cameron blinked. "Oh, he, erm — he doesn't really have anywhere else he wanted to go. He slept on a sofa bed at the dog rescue place on Sundays. I didn't know. I thought he was at a friend's or something. Then when his probation here was up, I kinda said he should move in permanently. He said he didn't mind keeping an eye on Em while you were here."

"Cam — should I be worried — is he taking

Deefur Dog

advantage — worse, are you taking advantage?"

Cameron blushed, he really did. He full-on blushed and Neal watched his brother thoughtfully. Cam twisted his hand into Deefur's soft fur as the dog leaned into him, fresh from the heat of the garden. "He loves Emma, loves it here. I'm happy he is here, Neal."

"Are you — ?" Neal didn't finish the sentence; simply gestured vaguely, wondering how else to put it.

"God, no." Cameron spluttered, and Neal joined him in looking out at the long-limbed man who had formed such an integral part of their lives. "Sometimes though…"

"Sometimes? Cameron?" Neal tilted his head to one side, glancing back and seeing the blush high on his brother's cheekbones. "You could do worse, dude," he added. "I like Jason."

"He's so young, Neal," Cameron whispered, almost to himself.

"He's what, four years younger than you? That's nothing."

"Four years, but so much younger in outlook than me. Mark was the one who led me, who pushed me. He was my older guy. I'm not sure I can be that for Jason, even if he wasn't my employee."

Neal looked puzzled. He didn't get the whole dynamic of Cameron's relationship with Mark. Neal only remembered how Mark appeared to be the... confident one, the one who made decisions. Cameron never questioned anything. He and Mark had a settled, happy relationship, and Neal often observed how Cam would go with the flow for the most part. If Cameron didn't think he could be that man for Jason, if he believed Jason needed an older, experienced, confident guy as a partner, then maybe he should stay away from Jason completely.

"I see a lot there," Neal pointed out. He sipped his black coffee and cursed when the liquid burned his tongue. Maybe he'd said too much. When he had started the conversation, he wanted to be sure Cameron was hands-off, wanted to know Jason wasn't taking Cameron for a ride. He didn't expect to be sitting here pushing his brother into a lifetime of domestic bliss (or even a hot session of no-holds-barred sweaty sex), with his nanny.

"Problem is, Neal — " Cameron sighed, turning back to the papers, knuckling his eyes. "I think maybe I see a lot there too."

Neal looked at his brother's lowered head. "Does it scare you?"

Deefur Dog

Quickly, Cameron raised his eyes and they were filled with indecision. "You can't begin to know how scared I am that I'll fuck this up."

* * * *

Neal had left and the cubey-climby thing was built, a twist and click of red and yellow with a slide that Emma now climbed up, as opposed to sliding down. Jason took photos with Cameron's digital camera as he promised he would, and laughed hysterically as Deefur tried to join in. Just as Cameron walked out to join them, the massive dog caught Jason off-balance. He ended up flat on the ground, Deefur's huge paws on his chest, and reached up a hand in a plea for help.

Cameron stood above him, looking down. "You all having fun, guys?" he asked and Emma jumped squealing from the cube into her daddy's arms, her scent a mix of grass and sun screen and little girl.

"Daddy, J finished," she declared, her voice nearly an octave higher than normal, her face flushed with excitement.

"I see, Pumpkin, is it good?"

"See, Daddy." She wriggled down, climbing

up the slide again and standing on the flat top,
waving her chubby arms and jumping up and
down on the spot. Deefur barked at the sudden
noise but got quiet when Jason shushed him.
Emma slid down the slide to bump onto the
grass before picking herself up and running after
her dog.

"Did you get it all done?" Jason asked
conversationally, lying back on the grass.

"Yeah, all sorted. Looks like you had fun
out here." Cameron lay down next to his nanny,
the warmth and relaxation of a job well done
flooding through him along with the late
afternoon rays. Sighing, he rolled to one side to
face Jason, supporting his head on one bent arm.
"Neal asked why you were here today." He didn't
have to elaborate; Jason understood what
Cameron said. Neal, after three months, had
finally decided to comment on the openly gay
nanny working for the openly gay father. "I told
him the truth. You did it to help me out."
Cameron said firmly. Jason pushed himself to
stand, offering a hand and pulling Cameron to
his feet in a swift move. The two men ended up
mere inches apart. Cameron looked up, acutely
aware of the four inches Jason had on him, of the
bulk he had on him, the complete physical
presence of Jason, and again he got the same heat

Deefur Dog

he always felt around the younger man. He suspected Jason sensed it too. Jason didn't let go and let his long, strong fingers twist into Cameron's, refusing to relinquish the grip.

"Jason," he eventually said softly, pulling his hand away and stepping back, "join us for dinner? Thought I'd grill a few steaks, make a salad and stuff. Be ready at six?"

* * * *

This was new. The Sunday evening meal was the only meal they didn't usually share. Usually Cameron-Emma time, the unspoken rule allowed for Jason to go to his own side of the house, now that he didn't go to Billy's on a Sunday to sleep. This assumption gave Cameron time alone with his daughter. Jason often escaped the house with Deefur just to get away from his own envious thoughts.

"I'd love to. I'm — gonna get a shower, then." Jason offered, glancing back at Emma, Cameron's responsibility now. Nothing else to do but to walk to his own private door and sit numbly on the side of his bed, looking around his small room, and wondering what the fuck Neal had said to Cameron. Or more importantly, what

Cameron had said to Neal.

He showered, washing away the outdoors, the grass and the sun and the sweat, sprayed deodorant and cologne sparingly, and crossed to his closet. He pulled out his only pair of clean jeans and grimaced, they weren't exactly designer, and were worn on the left knee. Sighing, he put them on and buttoned the fly, tightened the belt, and then inspected his piss-poor collection of shirts. Finally he picked out a black button down, pushed his arms through the sleeves, and slipped each button carefully through the holes, his fingers suddenly too clumsy, too big, for the tiny fastenings.

Finally he combed those same fingers through his damp hair and, half an hour early, slumped down on the bed and waited.

He managed to while away the time scribbling notes in his head on his final dissertation. Listening to the noise from the other bathroom meant Cameron had taken a shower as well. Finally enough time had passed making it seem reasonable to stroll casually into the kitchen as if he hadn't been waiting for ages. He had a whole string of interesting things he could talk about stored in his head ready to go, clever, important, current-affairs type subjects, but the minute he laid eyes on Cameron, every single

Deefur Dog

intelligent comment fled his mind.

Cameron wore jeans and a green shirt, the sleeves pushed back as he worked on making a green salad, the steaks already put to one side for the grill. He looked up as Jason entered the room, and it was all Jason could do not to kiss him hello. Cameron's hair, still damp from the shower, lay in soft spikes, his blue eyes framed with dark lashes, and his lips slightly parted in an open, friendly smile. Beautiful.

Jason thought maybe there could be something between them. Maybe this could grow into more than the simple attraction he felt for Cameron. Admitting this, if only to himself, was damned scary.

Cameron had never looked as good as this to Jason, never quite so — *shit* — kissable. It made him want to hoist him up on the counter, daughter or not, and take his fill of those lips; stand closer, push him over the edge. The intensity of his feelings caught him by surprise and he coughed, hoping against hope his loose shirt covered his instant freaking hard-on. He sat in his assigned chair opposite Emma and started talking to her, trying to focus on what she said rather than, every so often, looking up at Cameron and having to will the lust away.

"Can I help?" he asked Cameron softly, who waved away the offer with a soft, "No, stay sitting," and a beer, and yeah, he was happy to sit and watch as Cameron grilled and moved and did 'stuff'. This felt different tonight; it felt strange, new, almost like a date. The affection had been growing, hand in hand with the need, and the lust and the confusion and tumble of love would not stay hidden tonight. Jason bet he wore the expression on his face like a flag.

Hey Cameron, the flag said, I think I love you —

The meal was lovely, the conversation good, and when Emma was in bed, the two men sat on the sofa and watched a rerun of *Die Hard* for what Jason imagined to be his fiftieth time. He never got tired of it, and he would never get tired of quiet time with *his* Cameron.

Deefur Dog

Chapter 9

Christmas came and went with nothing said, nothing acted on, but Jason's sensitivity allowed him to notice Cameron's gradual slide into a kind of closed-off introspection. Jason guessed why. He wasn't stupid. The second anniversary of Mark's death approached, if he remembered right. He recalled Cameron saying something about January. He didn't know, or ask about, the exact date, just gave himself one hundred and ten percent as a buffer between any stress in the house and Cameron.

Jason heard the deep, heartfelt sobs from the kitchen on a normal Friday lasting late into the night, the house otherwise quiet as Emma and Deefur slept on. Jason hesitated for a good long while, until the crying stopped. He didn't want to intrude, but he could hear his momma's voice, *hot chocolate for the midnight chills would be good*, and quietly he moved down the hall and into the small kitchen. Cameron sat at the breakfast bar, his head in his hands and a bottle of whisky, unopened, in front of him.

Jason didn't say anything, just heated and poured milk over the powder in two mugs. He swapped one for the glass tumbler and bottle in front of Cameron and slid onto the stool next to his boss. They sat for a good half hour in silence, sipping hot chocolate, each lost in their own thoughts, until eventually Cameron stood, shaky and pale, placed the dirty mug in the sink, and leaned back against the counter. Jason stayed put, looking up thoughtfully as Cameron sighed.

"He was such a good person, you know," Cameron began, his throat raw from tears.

"Tell me," Jason said simply.

And Cameron did.

"I loved him, from the moment we met. So confident, so happy all the time... He had a head full of dreams and a heart full of love..."

Jason listened to everything, the highs and the lows, Emma, Deefur, the night Mark died, the impossible grief that had circled Cameron's heart ever since. Right there, in the kitchen, with Cameron wanting to talk, Jason fell in love so deeply and irrevocably, there would be no way out.

He never wanted to find a way out.

* * * *

As Emma's third birthday approached, the

Deefur Dog

tension between Cameron and Jason ramped to a higher level. Cameron's parents wanted quality time with their granddaughter, and whisked her away for a birthday trip to Disney, the trigger for everything to finally go wrong, or right, whichever way you looked at the situation.

"Bye, baby. Be good now for Gramma and Gramps," Cameron whispered into Emma's ear as he buckled her into the car seat.

"I will, Daddy," she said softly, her head focusing on Disney princesses and Minnie Mouse.

As he stood waving, watching the car leave the street, he felt suddenly unbearably lonely and found his feet wouldn't move. Deefur sensed an issue and pushed a cold wet nose into Cameron's hand, forcing the man to look down and focus on the big brown eyes looking up at him. Deefur let out a low whine and turned to go back in the house. Cameron followed, pulled the gate shut, and climbed the steps to the porch. He wondered where Jason was, and why he hadn't waved goodbye in the front yard. He went in search of the younger man, finally coming across him in Emma's room, folding clothes and tidying.

"Hey," Cameron said, causing Jason to jump a mile in the air and turn with a significant flush

98

RJ Scott

of sadness on his face.

"Hey," he said simply in return, dropping the last of the tiny shirts onto the folded pile and sighing. "Two weeks, Cameron, two freaking weeks."

"You decided if you're going home?" Cameron asked in conversation, not wanting to focus on the fact his baby would be gone for two whole weeks.

"Home?" Jason said, "To Mom and Dad? Nah, I'm gonna be looking after Deefur, staying here, getting some studying in. Finals are in a few weeks." Carefully he moved past Cameron and out of the room. "If that's okay with you?" he tagged on.

"Jeez, no, stay — I mean it's cool, if you want to stay." He sounded odd. He could hear it in his voice, and he searched desperately for something normal to say. "I'm gonna put in some pizza, maybe watch the game. You wanna keep me company?"

Jason's eyes widened almost comically. "God yeah, I'll get the beer."

* * * *

Their team won. Cause for celebration,

Deefur Dog

cause for more beer, and for sloppy slouching on Cameron's oversized couch, the evidence of pizza on plates cast to one side on the low table, and soft drawls as tiredness started to pull both men towards sleep.

" — and then, she only went and read the book straight off, I mean, no practice, nothing — " Jason was retelling a story from his class of five year olds he worked with on their reading, " — so the teacher sits there, blown away, and I am like 'yeah'." He pumped his fist in the air. "Score one for Everson and the child who refused to read." Falling back on the couch, he started to chuckle softly.

Cameron smiled. The alcohol clearly loosened Jason's tongue. His successes with the reading group were not something he bragged about normally, but Cameron wanted to hear everything.

He listened, watching Jason's lips form each word, ghosting syllables as he explained about his work, his hands flying to underscore his successes, his shoulders dropping in acknowledgement of his defeats. Every facet of Jason fascinated Cameron, but still at the back of his head lurked his doubt about whether he could be the experienced older man for Jason. Cameron wasn't a pushover, he had expectations

RJ Scott

in what he wanted in a relationship, but in bed he happily relaxed into whatever his lover wanted. He liked the more passive role, no, he craved it, and that had been fine with Mark, absolutely fine.

He squirmed as he listened to Jason's voice, realizing his fixating on the younger man, made him imagine things he shouldn't be thinking about, things that made him hard and needy for the first time in such a long time. Well, not exactly the first time. He had been doing this for a few months now, ever since the whole cubey-climby afternoon and his discussion with Neal. He sighed.

"Wow, a deep sigh," Jason commented. "You missing Em?"

Cameron nodded. Yes, he missed Emma. This was only the second time she'd been away from him, and this would be the longest time they had been apart.

"Yeah. I mean not what I'm thinking about, but yeah, I miss her." And there it was, out in the open, ready for Jason to ask him what he had actually been thinking about, or not. They sat quietly for a few seconds, Jason rolling his bottle between long, capable fingers, before placing the bottle on the table and turning to face Cameron.

Deefur Dog

He drew a leg under him, his hand along the back of the couch.

"So tell me — why the sigh? What were you thinking about? Work? Is everything okay?"

"Work? Yeah, our new project. Neal says we need to recruit another group of laborers so, yeah, well, I guess. It wasn't work, Jason."

Jason raised his eyebrows and leaned forward a few inches, listening carefully, waiting, ever attentive to what Cameron said. "I was thinking about you, actually."

"Me?"

"You and me, to be completely accurate. You and me and the whole employer-employee relationship and the fact that..." He paused, wanting to word this the right way, but aware he was crap at this and had so much to lose. "I think — I can't do this. I can't be the boss here. I don't know if I am saying this right — I mean maybe I am misinterpreting the whole thing — " As he spoke Jason leaned closer, until very gently the younger man cupped Cameron's face with a large hand, touching his lips to Cameron's in a soft press.

"Has anyone ever told you that you talk too much?" Jason said simply, curling his hand around the back of Cameron's neck and pulling

102

him closer, angling his head to run the tip of his tongue over Cameron's bottom lip. Cameron could taste beer and pizza, and the press of Jason's tongue asking for entrance. Sighing with the need for more, Cameron relaxed and opened his mouth to deepen the kiss. Jason took the initiative and sat higher to push Cameron down into the cushions. The kisses grew more heated, open-mouthed exchanges of breath, tasting, touching and learning.

The kissing and the touching felt so natural, so right, and told Cameron exactly what he had to do. Or say. He pulled back to whisper two words: "You're fired."

Jason smirked and leaned back, putting both feet flat on the floor. Then he lifted Cameron onto his lap with so little effort, iron went immediately to Cameron's dick, and suddenly he was so fucking hard. Grinding down, he heard Jason groan. He repeated the motion, finding an instinctive rhythm as they kissed. Jason pressed hard against him with one hand on Cameron's ass and one on his spine, stretching and pulling him to align so perfectly, Cameron could come here and now.

So much for worrying about taking the lead. Jason represented exactly what Cameron wanted, what he needed, and it was all he could

Deefur Dog

do not to come like a teenager there and then. Jason thrust and pushed and guided, rutting up against Cameron, sliding a hand up to twist into his short hair, moving his mouth to kiss-bite down on Cameron's neck, sucking and marking, words of passion in his voice, and words of need.

Cameron's spine melted. He whined against the onslaught, swore as Jason pulled his t-shirt up to his chin, clever fingers finding Cameron's hard nipples and pinching lightly. Then Jason pushed the t-shirt up and over Cameron's head, lifting his own top over his own head until skin met skin.

"Cameron, can we—" Jason eased Cameron down for another kiss, "—move this to the bedroom?"

Cameron barely heard him. Jason raised him up and off his lap, bringing them both to their feet. He caught both of Cameron's hands into one of his, holding them in a light hold, and Cameron recognized the promise in his eyes. Together, they moved to the stairs, exchanging kisses but saying nothing, their touches enough to communicate. Cameron found it difficult to find the way, difficult to track the walls, to turn the corner and enter his room, the only place in the house Jason had never entered. Then they were inside the door, both of them breathing

RJ Scott

heavily. With gentle strength loosening every joint Cameron possessed, Jason steered him until Cameron rested flat against the wall, his hands captured again and held above his head. To Cameron, this felt as right as it had with Mark, as perfect, as simple, more so maybe. As Jason kissed and tasted and stopped Cameron's ability to breathe, *this* was primal, and Cameron couldn't even begin to imagine not touching Jason, not having Jason.

* * * *

Jason groaned low in his throat, half-carrying Cameron to the bed, tugging at jeans and boxers, shoving his own down, until they lay naked and warm on the cool sheets, and then Jason stopped. He didn't want the speed or the heat, not straight away. He wanted this to be forever, this first time, wanted it to be special. So he slowed down, letting the tension run through every muscle in his new lover's body.

Resting his forehead on Cameron's chest, he laid a simple kiss on heated skin, and then rose to his knees, starting a kiss-trail south. Cameron's hands flexed in his hair, tight and then releasing, the pinch of pain lost in the lust to taste. The

Deefur Dog

teasing trail circled Cameron's groin and Jason's hands on Cameron's hips held him still as he ran his tongue over and around Cameron's cock, drawing him into his mouth and sucking him down.

It didn't take much. No way could this first time last, it had been so long in happening, and with Jason's clever lips and tongue, Cameron's breath stuttered in his throat with broken pleas of his lover's name. Jason pulled back, replacing mouth and tongue with one of his hands, and heard his own name groaned as Cameron arched up, tense and wired, losing it hot between them. Cameron still shuddered through the aftershocks as he reached for his bedside drawer, grabbing at bottles and condoms, scattering them this way and that on the bed. Jason's overwhelming desire to simply fuck this man into the mattress got pushed to one side by wanting to make love for the rest of the night. He leaned back and read the unspoken request in dark eyes: Please.

Encouraging Cameron to turn on his stomach, being better this way after such a long time, Jason coated his hand and fingers with slick. Kissing hot, biting kisses onto Cameron's lower spine, Jason's clever fingers opened his lover up, slowly and carefully, so wet with lubricant, he hoped Cameron felt little

RJ Scott

discomfort. He had been on the receiving end enough times to know the burn, to feel the pain, and he didn't want to hurt Cameron. He wanted this to be perfect. He moved slowly, watching in awe as Cameron pushed back on his fingers, two, and then three, taking his time, leaning forward to kiss the back of Cameron's neck. So slowly. Jason moved his fingers, encouraging the muscle to relax and open, until Cameron's incoherent pleas told him it was time. Jason wiped slick hands on the sheet, grabbing at the nearest condom and sheathing himself. Before he lost his control just at the sight of Cameron waiting, he lined himself up and slowly, carefully, entered. Cameron tensed at the breach and sucked in his breath as Jason moved further and gave a final, single-word appeal to fuck him.

The most precious gift Jason had ever received happened when this man arched his back against him. Cameron reacted vocally and physically, words tumbling from his mouth, of need and want and *fuck, right there*. Jason's own orgasm rose swiftly; he'd been so close when he first brought Cameron off with his mouth and hand alone. Resting back on his heels, he pulled Cameron up with him, his lover's back to Jason's chest, and long, capable hands reached around to counter the increasingly erratic and powerful

Deefur Dog

thrusts. Cameron was hard in his hands after only a short while. Could Cameron come again?

"Can you — *nghuh* — " He was so close — he wanted Cameron to —

He heard the mewl in Cameron's voice, the tension in his body, and Jason drove in strong and hard, sliding over that gland on each pass, while his fingers brushed over the head of Cameron's dick. Jason felt the stutter breath of orgasm and twisted his hand, and for the second time, Cameron was coming under his touch. Burying his face in Cameron's neck, Jason peaked, the erotic slide of cum on his hands, the breathless, half sobs from Cameron, even as Jason convulsed into orgasm in the most intense experience of his life.

They stayed still, until Jason realized he held a semi-conscious lover and he eased out, supporting Cameron down to lie flat. Then he removed the condom and discarded it, smiling as Cameron shifted to face him. Cameron's eyes were shut, long lashes fanning on blushed, freckled skin, and the sight of him filled all the spaces in Jason's heart. With exhaustion claiming him too, he slid to lie down, his face inches from Cameron's, and pulled the covers over them both. They needed to sleep, but there was one thing he really needed to say.

RJ Scott

"Why did we wait so long?"

* * * *

Cameron woke first, wincing at the ache in his ass and smiling at the enormity of what had happened the night before. For want of better wording, it really had been a long time coming.

"Coffee?" Jason pleaded from under the covers. All that showed of him was the tangle of dark hair against the white sheets. Cameron put on boxers, padding down to the kitchen, letting a yawning Deefur into the garden, and then returning to the bedroom with two coffees and toast. Nervous apprehension twisted in his stomach; he wondered what this morning would be like, the morning after, half of him scared Jason would leave, half of him scared he would stay. He placed the coffee on the side table and sat down carefully, his hands pressed over his belly, willing the churning to subside and wondering if coffee would help or hinder. He startled when a warm hand covered one of his, and a trail of warm kisses traced the base of his spine. He didn't want to move, but Jason grasped his hand and climbed out of bed, led him to the bathroom, and proceeded to grab a spare

Deefur Dog

toothbrush, mumbling something along the lines of "teeth, bed". Cameron got with the plan and brushed his teeth, catching Jason looking at him in the mirror, making him blush like a teenager.

"Is Deefur okay?" Jason asked around a mouthful of minty bubbles.

"I put him in the garden, he's fine."

"We'll walk him after... yeah?" Jason didn't sound uncertain, wasn't questioning anything, even used the word after.

"Yeah," Cameron replied softly, "maybe the lake?"

When they finished rinsing, Jason captured his hand again and towed him back to the bed, both laughing as Cameron lost his balance and tumbled in an ungraceful sprawl on untidy bedclothes. Jason started the awkward conversation by putting together enough thoughts to say something rational and changed the course of the morning with a few words.

"Is it okay for me to say I love you, now?" he began tentatively, "and I love Emma like she is my own, and that I even love Deefur?"

Cameron blinked; those were not the words he had been expecting.

"More than okay," he finally said, "I think it's safe to say we love you too."

RJ Scott

* * * *

Emma jumped down out of the car and ran into her daddy's arms, raining kisses on his face and talking about everything; princesses and Mickey and rides and bedrooms and her cousin Anna whom she loved and —

Cameron just gripped tight, his mom and dad following him into the house. Jason retreated to the kitchen, commanding Deefur to follow him, which the huge hairy menace did with a docile trot across the tiles. Cameron could see him through the open door, fiddling with the coffee filter, obviously afflicted by a sudden urge to hide in the face of Cameron's family.

"J!" Emma shouted happily, wriggling to be put down and half climbing Jason until he swung her up in his arms and allowed kisses with a stupid grin on his face. She clambered back down, burying her face and fingers into Deefur's fur. Deefur immediately rolled on his back exposing his belly for a rub and Jason crouched down to talk to Emma, asking her questions about her holiday.

"That dog loves Jason," Cameron's mom said gently.

Deefur Dog

"He does." He wanted to shout that he loved Jason as well, but maybe that should wait Selfishly he wanted to keep that knowledge to himself just for a few more days..

Cameron leaned into his mom as she put an arm around his waist and squeezed. She watched Jason with her granddaughter, and Cameron realized she could probably see the love between nanny and daughter as plain as the nose on her face.

"I heard hundreds of Jason stories from Emma when we were away." She smiled up at him as she said this.

"You did?"

"About how Deefur was going to a new family, and about mashed carrots, and tomatoes, and walks, and slide building. I think my granddaughter loves Jason as much as Deefur does."

"I know."

"Cam darling?" she paused and then leaned her head against his arm, "he's a special person."

"I know mom, it's just, mom…" he knew he sounded helpless, his gaze going back to his small family roughhousing on the kitchen floor. Mark had been such a defined part of him, was still in his heart. Could it work to make room for

RJ Scott

someone else? "How can I…" His mom squeezed his arm gently.

"Are you thinking of Mark?" she said simply, and Cameron pulled his hand out to return the hug. It was enough. Simple words to make him think. Mark would have loved Jason, would have wanted to be there for Emma and Deefur, but when he couldn't be, then Jason would have been his choice. Cameron knew that. Deep inside his heart there would always be love for Mark, but now it seemed entirely possible that he had a new space just for Jason.

"Cam, you know that Mark would have liked Jason."

"Yes." Cameron nodded, his throat tight with emotion, "yes, he would."

The End

Deefur Dog

About the Author

RJ Scott lives just outside London. She has been writing since age six, when she was made to stay in at lunchtime for an infraction involving cookies and was told to write a story. Two sides of A4 about a trapped princess later, a lover of writing was born. She loves reading anything from thrillers to sci-fi to horror; however, her first real love will always be the world of romance. Her goal is to write stories with a heart of romance, a troubled road to reach happiness, and more than a hint of happily ever after.

Email: rj@rjscott.co.uk
Webpage: www.rjscott.co.uk
Facebook: author.rjscott
Twitter: rjscott_author

Love Lane Books

Lovelanebooks.co.uk is a UK based publisher of gay romantic fiction.

Deefur Dog

Other RJ Scott books in paperback

The Christmas Throwaway
The Decisions We Make
The Gallows Tree
New York Christmas
The Heart Of Texas
Texas Winter *(Texas 2)*
Texas Heat *(Texas 3)*
Guarding Morgan *(Sanctuary 1)*
The Only Easy Day *(Sanctuary 2)*
Face Value *(Sanctuary 3)*
Still Waters *(Sanctuary 4)*
Full Circle *(Sanctuary 5)*
The Journal Of Sanctuary One *(Sanctuary 6)*
World's Collide *(Sanctuary 7)*
Oracle
Book Of Secrets *(Oracle book 2)*

With Meredith Russell
Follow The Sun *(Sapphire Cay book 1)*
Under The Sun *(Sapphire Cay book 2)*
The Art Of Words

Made in the USA
Charleston, SC
22 June 2015